LLOYD VS. LORD GARMADON

ADAPTED BY KATE HOWARD

SCHOLASTIC INC.

ISBN 978-1-338-26433-3

10 9 8 7 6 5 4 3 2 1   18 19 20 21 22

Printed in the U.S.A.   40

First printing 2018

A TIME OF PEACE

For the first time in months, Ninjago City felt safe.

The ninja had saved their city from the Sons of Garmadon. Most of the gang was in prison. And the group's leader, Princess Harumi, was under arrest.

The ninja had a party to celebrate their victory. They sang and relaxed and had some fun.

But deep down, the ninja knew the fun wouldn't last long. Their enemies were always planning their next move.

The Sons of Garmadon were in jail. And Lord Garmadon was still in the Departed Realm.

But Lloyd knew that his father never stayed missing for long. He had to be ready to face Garmadon if his father ever returned.

JAILBREAK

The ninja soon discovered their worst fears were coming true.

Harumi had broken out of jail — and someone had helped her escape.

The police believed it was Lord Garmadon!

The ninja hurried to police headquarters.

"Are you *sure* it was Lord Garmadon?" Zane asked.

"Yes," the police chief said. "But it's like they brought back the worst parts of him. Twenty of my officers tried to take him down. But we couldn't stop him."

"Well," Cole told Lloyd, "at least it's just your father and Harumi. The other Sons of Garmadon are still locked up."

Just then, there was breaking news. Someone had broken into Kryptorium Prison!

"Well, I guess we now know where Harumi and Lord Garmadon are," Zane said.

At the prison, the warden offered Harumi a deal. "Okay, y-you and all your friends are free to go. No one needs to get hurt, right?"

Harumi smiled. "Actually, I think we're going to stay. In fact, if anyone's leaving —" With that, she pushed the warden and all his guards out the door.

LORD GARMADON RETURNS

"The ninja will be coming for us," Harumi told her sidekick, UltraViolet. "Get ready."

Then Harumi opened all the jail cells. "Sons of Garmadon!" she shouted. "No longer shall I be silent, and no longer shall you be silent. Our father has returned!"

Harumi bowed toward the door. The gang members stepped back in awe.

A huge figure entered the prison cellblock: Lord Garmadon.

He was back. And he was more evil looking than ever before!

Meanwhile, the ninja had boarded the *Destiny's Bounty*. They were on their way to the prison, and they were ready to fight.

"This is not good," Cole told the team. "This is *really* not good."

"You barely beat them last time," Pixal told the ninja.

Zane nodded. "And that was when we had help from the entire police force!"

"Now they have Lord Garmadon on their side," Nya said.

Lloyd stared at a photo of him and his father. He gritted his teeth.

Lloyd knew what he had to do. He had to try to get his father back.

"We must go to Kryptorium Prison," he told the team.

"Okay . . ." Jay said. "So we take on Garmadon, Harumi, AND her entire gang? Not your best idea."

Lloyd took a deep breath. "I have to face him. I turned him good once. I can do it again."

"Uh," Kai said. "That sounds like a *really* bad idea."

"I agree. It's too dangerous. That is exactly what they want you to do," Zane said. "I believe your past may be clouding your judgment, Lloyd."

All the other ninja agreed with Zane.

Lloyd sighed. "Okay, then what do we do?"

Inside the prison, Lord Garmadon was practicing his fight moves. He battled each of the Sons of Garmadon. He easily beat them all.

"Good," Harumi told him. "Your strength has returned. You have the power to create . . . and destroy."

Harumi smiled. "You can unlock your true potential, Garmadon," she said. "A *dark* potential. But you must overcome the one obstacle that has always stood in your way: Lloyd."

Garmadon's face grew angry. "Then bring him to me."

Harumi smiled. "I won't have to. He will come."

MAN WITH A PLAN

Back on the *Destiny's Bounty*, Lloyd had a plan. If the other ninja didn't want to face Garmadon, he would go alone.

Lloyd knew his friends would try to stop him. So he locked the ninja inside the ship's galley.

"Lloyd, what are you doing? Open this door!" Nya screamed.

"I'm sorry," said Lloyd. "I have to confront him. It's something I have to do — alone."

Lloyd raced through the ship. He grabbed a parachute pack and strapped it to his back.

It was time to face his father.

Lloyd jumped off the *Destiny's Bounty* and climbed into his Green Racer.

Cole, Jay, Kai, Nya, and Zane were determined to escape. They couldn't let Lloyd face Garmadon alone.

"Stand back, guys," said Cole. His fists began to glow. He slammed them against the locked door.

BOOM! The ninja were free.

The ninja raced toward the control room, but Lloyd was gone.

"He's in his car," Cole said, studying the control board. "He's heading toward the prison!"

FATHER VS. SON

Harumi watched on a prison monitor as Lloyd's Green Racer sped toward the entrance.

The Green Ninja fired missiles to blast open the doors. But it wasn't necessary. Harumi opened the gates for him. She wanted Lloyd to fight Garmadon.

"Father!" Lloyd screamed. "Come out and face me!"

Harumi turned to her team. "Are we filming this? Broadcast it to the world. Let them see what true power looks like."

Harumi's henchman Killow clicked a few buttons. A moment later, Lloyd's meeting with Garmadon was playing on every TV in Ninjago City.

Inside the *Destiny's Bounty*, Nya gasped. Lloyd had appeared on her computer screen.

"What's with Lloyd on the TV?" Cole asked.

Kai's eyes went wide. "Harumi . . . She *wants* us to watch."

Lloyd walked into the empty cellblock. The door swung shut behind him.

"It was foolish to come here," Garmadon growled.

Before Lloyd could respond, Garmadon launched his attack.

"I didn't come to fight you," Lloyd said, dodging. "My father is somewhere in there. I've saved you once, I'll save you again."

"THERE IS NOTHING LEFT TO SAVE!" Garmadon howled.

"Listen to me," Lloyd said. "You don't have to do this. Harumi is using you as a pawn."

"You are the pawn," Garmadon shouted. "A pawn to your own foolish hopes!"

Garmadon blasted Lloyd. The Green Ninja flew backward and landed in a heap on the floor. Garmadon hit him again and again.

"Yes," Harumi said, smiling as she watched the fight on her monitor. "He's finding it. His true potential!"

Lloyd had no choice. He had to fight back.

Both father and son fought as hard as they could.

Lloyd called up his remaining strength. But it wasn't enough. Garmadon's power was too much for him.

With a final, powerful blast, Garmadon threw Lloyd through the prison wall.

It was over. Lloyd was alive . . . but defeated. Garmadon had won!

"Gather everyone," Harumi told her gang with an evil grin. "We ride to the city at dawn. It's time Ninjago City meets their new Emperor . . . Emperor GARMADON!"